Channing O'Banning

and the

Rainforest Rescue

By Angela Spady

Illustrated by Tammie Lyon

Santa Cruz Press

Copyright@ 2013

Channing O'Banning and the Rainforest Rescue by Angela Spady
Illustrations by Tammie Lyon
Published in the United States of America by Santa Cruz Press
www.channingobanning.com

Summary: Channing fears she's lost her best friend to the new
boy at school and learns more about the rainforest than she'd
ever imagined.

ISBN-13: 978-0-61577-3995
ISBN-10: 0615773990

Library of Congress Control Number: 2013901879
Santa Cruz Press
Leburn, KY

To C.E.E.
For showing me all of
the possibilities with a pencil.

Table of Contents

Snap Out of It!

Summer vacation was only a few weeks away, but none of my teachers seemed to notice. I was up to my eyeballs in homework. My brain was turning into jello. Even my locker smelled like old cheese. I kept forgetting to take home my lunch box, and green fuzzies were growing on my old sandwich crumbs. School break couldn't get here fast enough!

"Remember class, there will be a quiz tomorrow," said Mr. Doring, our science teacher. "You MUST know how plants help our environment!"

That was the *third* time he'd reminded us today. No wonder we called him Boring Doring. He was about to drive me bonkers. Who needed to know about a bunch of science junk, anyway?

Art was the only class that I liked. After all, I AM an artist and will be world famous someday. It's only a matter of time before my drawings will be in a museum. I'll probably be forced to wear sunglasses and hide from all of my fans. Luckily, I keep a pencil stashed in my ponytail, just in case I need to give an autograph or draw something cool. But for now, I was in science class. YUCK.

"He must think we're totally clueless," I whispered to Maddy, my best friend.

I wasn't sure she'd heard me.

"He's reminded us ten zillion times about that goofy quiz. Why are we having a test this time of the year, anyway?" I said a little louder.

"Uh, right...Chan... clueless test...a zillion times...uh yeah...yeah."

Huh? What was her problem?

Every word I'd said had gone through one ear and out the other. Maybe Boring Doring had finally pushed her over the edge.

Maybe she'd turned into a science zombie?

I pulled my Lime Lizard Green pencil from my ponytail and dropped it onto the floor on purpose. I needed to check out what Maddy was doing at her desk. If she'd really turned into a zombie, I should probably run for my life!

And then I saw it.

Maddy was in a total daze and writing in her notebook: Maddy + Marco 4 Ever.

Ugh.

This was all Cooper's fault. No, really it was ALL Marco Ramos's fault!

Marco was the new kid at school. Well, he wasn't *that* new. He'd been here for almost a month and seemed like any other fourth grade boy to me. We didn't know much about him, only that he spoke Spanish and English, and that his dad was looking for a new job.

But yesterday Marco told Cooper that he thought Maddy was cute, and of course, Coop had to run straight and tell Maddy. Cooper Newberry is one of my best friends, but he blabs everything to the entire planet. And now, thanks to the big mouth, Maddy had gone goofy in science class--all because of a boy.

"Helllloooo...earth to Maddy...come in for a landing...do you hear meeee???"

I snapped my fingers as loudly as possible, trying to get her attention.

Just when Maddy noticed I was alive, I felt our teacher standing right behind my desk. His stare was burning a hole into my ponytail.

"Miss Channing O'Banning, do YOU have something you'd like to tell the whole class?" Mr. Boring glared over top of his glasses, like one of those mad scientists on the sci fi channel.

"Uh...no...uh...sorry...sorry Mr. Boring," I said quickly.

The whole class cracked up.

"Oh! Oh! I mean Mr. Doring--NOT Mr. Boring--SIR!!" I corrected myself.

Cooper laughed so hard that I thought his head might blow off. His whole face turned red. Almost purple. *It wasn't that funny.*

But just when I was about to get the Boring Doring lecture on "No Talking While the Teacher is Talking," the bell rang for class to be over. YES! I couldn't leave science class fast enough.

"Way to go, Chan," Cooper griped. "The last thing we need is for Boring Doring to get mad at everyone on the last week of school. He could really make this test a doozy."

Secretly, I wanted to chew Cooper out for blabbing to Maddy what Marco had said about her. That's what started this whole thing in the first place. But I couldn't get too mad. Coop had been one of my best friends since kindergarten. He understood me better than anyone. Maddy understood me too, but now she was in Marco la la land.

"I don't see WHY we have to know so much about a bunch of dumb plants," I complained.

"Yeah, me either, but we still have to take the quiz, Chan. Otherwise, we'll flunk and have to take it again, next year."

Cooper did have a point. I couldn't face the future if Boring Doring was in it two years in a row. Coop always thought of things ahead of time, which is exactly why he was the smartest kid in class. He remembered to study for every single quiz and he always remembered to complete every assignment. Basically, Cooper was the exact opposite of me. I tried not to think about things that stunk, and science, to me, was one of the stinkiest things EVER. Cooper Newberry loved it. Apparently, so did Marco.

"I'll help you guys study for the quiz," said someone behind us. "I know a lot about plants and animals and stuff."

That's when I looked over my shoulder. *Ugh.* It was You-Know-Who.

Marco and Maddy were walking right behind us. I couldn't help but glance over at Cooper. He didn't seem to be as bugged about it as I was.

"Oh yeah?" I asked Marco. "Are you a plant and animal expert or something?"

I didn't need anyone's help...especially from Marco, the Best Friend Thief.

"We learned about all kinds of plants at my old school, in Costa Rica. There's every kind you can imagine in the rainforest. Some of the plants and animals don't exist anywhere else in the world."

I looked over at Maddy and she was grinning from ear to ear. She looked at Marco like he was some kind of genius. Her eyes almost rolled back into her brain.

I wanted to scream.

"We have zoos around here you know," I pointed out. "AND Planetariums!"

"Uh, Chan, planetariums study *planets*, not plants," Coop whispered.

Oh whatever!

"You may know something about plants, Marco, but I happen to know EVERYTHING about animals." I said.

Snap Out of It!

That was one thing I was sure about.
After all, I could draw *any* and *every* kind of
animal. I looked over at Cooper, hoping he'd
agree that I was an animal expert. I finally
had to poke him with my elbow to make sure
that he got the hint.

"OWWW! Yeah, Chan knows TONS about
animals and stuff," Cooper said.

I thought Maddy might speak up and
agree with Cooper, but no such luck. I doubt
if she even knew I was standing there.

"Have *you* ever seen a blue jean frog,
Channing O'Banning?" Marco asked.

I couldn't help but laugh. So did Cooper.
Marco must have thought we'd believe
anything.

"HA! HA! Yeah, right," I said. "I guess
you've seen purple elephants or giraffes that
wear sneakers too, huh?"

Everyone laughed at my comeback—everyone except Marco and Maddy, of course.

"Whatever, Channing O'Banning. Come on Maddy, let's get to class. Some people are just rude!"

Maddy zoomed around me and Cooper with her nose stuck up in the air. If the sprinkler system had gone off, she would have drowned. My EX-BEST FRIEND walked around with Mr. Plant Expert, acting like we didn't exist.

Oh why did that boy have to move to Greenville?!!

I couldn't wait to go home and get out my Candy Apple Red pencil and my secret sketchbook. I already knew what I was going to draw: a picture of Maddy with a big red X over her face.

Best Friends---WHO NEEDS THEM!

B.F.F.

I remember the very first time I met Madison Martinez, or "Maddy." Our preschool teacher had put our desks into alphabetical order. Since "Martinez" came before "O'Banning," Maddy sat right in front of me. She had the curliest brown hair of anyone I'd ever seen. And Maddy said she'd never seen a kid with as many freckles as I had. She asked if anyone had ever tried to connect the dots on my arms and legs. I tried that later, with a purple marker, and got into big trouble.

Once in preschool, when I was really bored, I slid a jumbo crayon into a curl on the back of Maddy's head. She didn't even notice it--- that is, until Cooper blabbed about it. I thought it looked good with her pink outfit, but Maddy didn't think so. She tattled on me to the teacher in two seconds. I had to stay in at recess and everything.

I drew a picture of a pink giraffe and told Maddy that I was really sorry. We've been best friends ever since---or HAD been best friends---until Marco Ramos came along.

Maddy and I always had fun at sleepovers, too. She took ballet lessons and would try to teach me a few of her moves. In exchange, I'd give Maddy a few drawing lessons and let her use my colored pencils. We soon decided to stick to what we liked best, though. My legs felt like pretzels when I tried standing in one of those ballet positions. And Maddy couldn't even draw a turtle, which seemed like the easiest thing in the world to me.

Sometimes we'd have a sleepover at my Nana O'Banning's house. She's the coolest grandmother on the planet and Maddy thinks so too. Maddy once brought over some old dance costumes from her ballet recitals. We even dressed up Teeny, my Nana's pot-bellied pig, in a pink tutu. He didn't seem to mind at all. Actually, I think he kind of liked it. Teeny twirled and twisted around like he was on a real stage. Nana even gave him a rose, but I can't remember if he smelled it or ate it.

But I looked weirder than Teeny. I felt silly in the pink tights and purple leotard that Maddy picked out for me. She even took the pencil out of my ponytail, and crammed a sparkly princess crown on my head. And the ballet shoes were horrible! They cramped my toes so bad that I could hardly walk. It took two whole days to straighten out my feet, so that I could wear my high top sneakers again.

Maddy was a natural ballerina. She could do leaps and stand on her tiptoes like it was the easiest thing in the world. She was the best dancer in the whole school.

It was going to be weird not having Maddy as one of my best friends. She probably wouldn't miss me at all. It was all Marco's fault.

After getting home from school and gobbling down a few gummy turtles, I tried not to think about Maddy. I had other stuff to worry about —like a dumb plant quiz!!

But for some reason, my brain was asleep. I couldn't concentrate on a single thing. Instead, I drew and doodled all over my science papers. I knew all of that plant stuff anyway. A flower grows from a seed. It needs water and sun. Bees get the pollen and take it to other plants. *Blah, blah, blah!*

I think Boring Doring was trying to make us all drop out of fourth grade. If only he'd remember that everyone isn't as excited about science as he is---everyone except Marco, that is. I still didn't get why he had to act like the world's greatest expert on plants and animals.

Weird. Very Weird.

Beware of Frogs Wearing Sneakers

Strawberry gummy turtles are the yummiest snack ever and I can't get enough of them. I keep them in my backpack, my bookshelf, and in a few places that I can't even say out loud. My big sister Katie thinks that gummies fry my brain, but what does she know. However, every time I eat them before bed, I have the craziest dreams.

Last night I dreamed that Marco was the star of a TV show about the jungle. He even wore a tan shirt and shorts like all of those other zoo people. He swung through the trees with a monkey on his shoulder, and fought a monster plant with giant arms and legs. I was in the dream too, and about to be eaten by a strange red frog wearing blue jeans. It even wore a pair of my high top sneakers! Just when I was about to become its lunch, I screamed out loud and woke up Katie.

"Hey loud mouth!" she yelled from across the hallway. "SOME people are trying to sleep around here! Did you forget it's Saturday morning? *Geez*!!"

What a relief to wake up, even if it was to hear my grouchy sister. I rubbed my eyes to snap out of it, and tried to go back to sleep. But it was no use. The only thing I saw when I closed my eyes, was that crazy monster plant.

I had to think of something else. I even tried studying for the science quiz. Maybe if I studied about normal sized plants, I might get bored and fall sleep.

But that was no help either.

I got out my sketchbook and drew the ginormous plant from my dream. Maybe if I drew one of the things that scared me, it might leave my brain a little. Sometimes that seemed to help. I slowly drew the giant green leaves, an orange center, and wavy petals that were bright purple. Then I picked out a pencil called Puppy Nose Pink. It was the exact color of my skin, minus all the freckles. I drew the arms and legs next, added scary-looking eyes, and sketched a mouthful of teeth. It was Marco's fault that I'd had such a crazy nightmare in the first place.

Suddenly, Katie barged into my room before I had a chance to hide my sketchbook.

"Ever heard of knocking?" I asked Katie the Pest. *Why was she bugging me?*

"Ever heard of NOT screaming in your sleep?!" she asked. "I think you woke up everyone on Darcy Street. It was just a dream, you big baby."

"Duh," I said, and went back to my drawing. Maybe if I just ignored her, she'd go away.

"Wow. What's with the freaky drawing you've got there?" Katie asked, glancing over at my sketchbook.

"Oh, it's nothing," I flipped over my drawing so she wouldn't stare.

"Nothing, bluffing! Since when did you start drawing weird stuff like that?" she asked.

"What are you, a detective?" I was tired of Katie asking so many questions.

"Whatever," she said, flopping down into my beanbag chair without asking. "I heard your class got a new kid from Mexico, or somewhere like that. Maybe you can brush up on those Spanish words that Mom makes us practice. What does he look like? Is he cute?"

"THAT does it!! Get OUT of my room, Katie! I'm tired of your crazy questions. And he's from Costa Rica---NOT Mexico! And I don't care what he looks like, or what he does, or ANYTHING!"

"Okay…okay…*touchy touchy*!" said Katie, rolling her eyes. "I think I'm onto something, huh?" She smiled like she knew some big secret.

I pushed Katie out of my room and locked the door.

I'd had it with the snoop and I was tired of talking about Marco Ramos. If I heard one more word about the "new kid," I think I might explode into a zillion pieces. All I wanted to do was relax on a Saturday morning and watch TV.

I pulled on my fuzzy robe and put my hair up into a ponytail. It had a zillion lumps and stray hairs sticking out, but I didn't care. It looked better once I stuck my Pookie Purple pencil in the top.

I could smell Mom's chocolate chip pancakes from upstairs, and could almost taste their gooey goodness. Since Mom loved sleeping in on Saturdays too, she rarely made pancakes, unless it was a special occasion. But it wasn't anyone's birthday, or Mom and Dad's anniversary. I slid down the stair rail and bumped into Dad, splattering his coffee a little. *Oops.*

"Well, good morning to you too," he said. "Did you sleep well?"

"Not really," I yawned. "I sort of had a bad dream last night."

"Uh oh, that's too bad. Want to talk about it?"

"No, I'm okay, it was just a dumb dream, no big deal," I sort of fibbed. "Those chocolate chip pancakes smell delicious!"

"As soon as everyone comes downstairs, your Mom and I have a super special announcement!"

Weird. Very weird. *What were they up to?*

All I could think about was spreading butter on my pancakes, and drowning them in yummy syrup. I was one bite away from chocolate heaven.

Katie finally made it to the kitchen. If only Mom and Dad would hurry up with their news. My stomach was doing backflips.

"Dear, would you like to tell the girls, or should I?" asked Mom, smiling from ear to ear.

What was with my parents? Had they been eating my school glue?

"Does everyone remember how hard I've been trying to find more help at the clinic?" asked Dad. "Things have gotten really busy and I could use another doctor to help out. Well TODAY IS THE DAY! I finally found someone!"

Was THAT the big news?

I was glad Dad found some help, but I had more important things to worry about---like chocolate chip pancakes! I crammed the biggest bite ever into my mouth.

"Dr. Ramos is a nice doctor that just moved to Greenville. I think he'll be a great addition to the clinic."

I choked on my pancake and spit it onto my plate.

RAMOS?! That was Marco's last name. It couldn't be. It just couldn't be!

"Hey, that's great news Dad! I bet he's from Costa Rica, isn't he?" asked Katie, sneakily smiling at me.

"Why yes, Katie. Yes he is. And Chan, I think his son is in your class. His name is Marlon...or Mark?"

I felt dizzy. This was not happening.

"It's Marco. Marco Ramos, Dad," I gulped and said. I wanted to wipe that smile right off Katie's face.

"Yes, that's it! You two will become great friends. I think we should invite them over for lunch tomorrow. We'll introduce ourselves a little more."

This was not happening.

"That's a great idea, dear! I'll call Mrs. Ramos today!" Mom chimed in.

This wasn't another silly dream-----IT WAS A REAL NIGHTMARE!

D for Doomed!

Dinner with the Ramos family went better than expected. Our parents talked about boring stuff and Katie kept waiting for me to say something stupid. Mom fixed spaghetti, so I stared at the meatballs instead of looking at Marco. He hardly spoke a word, which was fine by me. Maybe Marco figured out that I knew more about animals than he ever would!

Thanks to my quick thinking, I told Mom that I had a stomachache and needed to go to my room. Anyway, I had studying to do. I was going to ace Boring Doring's science quiz. That would show Mr. Plant Genius!

* * *

On Monday morning, Boring Doring could hardly wait to pass out the big quiz. It was almost like he wanted us to flunk! I read each question over and over, hoping the answers would pop into my brain. My hands were so sweaty that I could hardly hold my pencil. The quiz was HORRIBLE!

I was the last one to turn in my paper.

"That quiz STUNK!" said Cooper. "The drawing of those plant parts looked nothing like the one in our book. What did you think about it, Chan?"

Cooper freaked about every single test, which made no sense to me. Everyone knew that he was a brainiac and made a big fat A on everything. Sometimes that really bugged me.

"I'm not too worried about it," I fibbed. "It was a piece of cake."

My head was still spinning from trying to think up all of the answers. I could feel my heart beat between my ears.

"What did you think about the quiz, Marco?" Cooper asked.

Oh, why did we need his opinion on things?

"It wasn't too bad," said Marco. "My mom made me study extra hard. I even practiced labeling a plant drawing at home, just to make sure that I could do it."

Of course he did.

"I guess we'll find out soon enough," said Cooper. "Boring Doring's grading them during recess."

I'd have been happier if our teacher could have waited for a few days. Or maybe for a week...or an eternity!

"How do you think you did, Chan?" asked Maddy.

I was shocked that my ex-best friend was even talking to me. In the last few days Maddy and I had hardly spoken a word to each other.

It was all Marco's fault.

Just as I was about to answer Maddy's question, the bell rang for class to start. Boring Doring had our papers graded. *Gulp.*

This could be bad. This could be really *really* bad. Maybe I should ask to be excused and hide out in the bathroom? It would be just my luck that the school nurse would find me, and she'd call Dad. Then I'd be forced to take medicine that tasted like sewer water. No thank you.

Boring Doring walked up and down the rows of desks, handing back our papers. He usually wrote our scores at the top with a giant red marker. He wrote it so big that everyone in the entire room could see it. They could probably see it from Mars.

My mouth was so dry that I could barely swallow. I felt like I'd eaten an entire jar of peanut butter. Luckily, Boring Doring wrote our scores with a pencil this time. Otherwise, everyone in class would have seen the giant "D" on my paper.

I was DOOMED. I was going to be DEAD MEAT when I got home. Maybe if I'd studied a little more, instead of drawing in my sketchbook, I would have gotten a better grade. IT WAS ALL MARCO'S FAULT. If he hadn't told Cooper that he thought Maddy was cute, Maddy wouldn't be acting so crazy. *I* wouldn't have lost my best friend over a dumb boy, *I* wouldn't have gotten upset, *I* wouldn't have had a bad dream, and *I* wouldn't have drawn in my sketchbook, instead of studying for that goofy quiz. It was all Marco's fault.

Summer vacation, get me out of here!!

We're Doing *What?!*

Before Marco messed up everything, Maddy and I would walk to the bakery after school and get a cherry vanilla cupcake.

But now, Maddy's mom picked her up right after school. Even though I still walked by the bakery, I just couldn't go in. It wasn't the same without my best friend.

Instead, I went home and ate the next best thing: grilled cheese stuffed with pickles and potato chips. Nana O'Banning had shown me how to make it all by myself. It was her favorite too. She and Teeny were coming over for dinner and I couldn't wait to see the most adorable pig on earth. Maybe he'd cheer me up a little.

* * *

"Hey gang, time for dinner!" yelled Dad, "It's a special meal for some special news!"

What could he be up to this time?

"I don't even want to guess about this one," I told Katie, as we came downstairs. "The last time Dad had a surprise, it was about Dr. Ramos working at the clinic. This better not have anything to do with Marco!"

"Are you still upset with him? He's cool, Chan," said Katie. "You're just jealous that he likes Maddy Martinez."

"I am not! I am not! You don't know ANYTHING!"

Katie could be such a pain.

"Are you girls coming, or is all this food for me and Teeny?" said someone from the kitchen. I knew that voice anywhere!

"Hey Nana! Hi Teeny!" I said, running to give them both hugs. "Do you know what Dad's news is all about? Can you give me a hint?"

Nana winked and tugged at my ponytail. "He mentioned that it has something to do with summer vacation. I guess it will be a surprise for all of us!"

Anything about summer vacation WAS good news! Maybe we were going to the beach? Or maybe New York City! I could visit tons of art museums there. Teeny and I sat at the table and tried to be patient. We were both starving. I even heard Teeny's stomach growl. Or maybe it was mine.

But when Mom brought food to the table, I didn't recognize anything.

Weird. Very weird.

"I hope I fixed the recipes correctly," said Mom. "Mrs. Ramos gave them to me. It's what they eat in Costa Rica!"

NOT AGAIN.

"The chicken dish is Arroz Con Pollo with black beans and rice. Everyone has to try it," Mom insisted.

She'd also fixed something that looked like cooked bananas, which were still hot.

Cooked bananas? How could a kid eat cooked bananas?

I'd rather eat school cafeteria food.

"These are plantains, Channing," Mom said. "They're sort of like bananas, only better. At least try one. You know the rule."

Katie and I have to try at least one bite of anything new. Sometimes Mom's rule really stinks. Like NOW. I looked around to make sure that a trashcan was close by. I held my nose and took a bite of the chicken. It was spicy...but DELISH!!

I took a deep breath before trying the banana plantain thingies. This could be gross. This could be really *really* gross. I put the tiniest bite possible on my fork and touched my tongue to it. Then I took a teensy weensy bite...

YUM! Who knew that plantains could be so tasty!

Teeny decided to brave it too. Nana filled his bowl with the Costa Rican food and he went bonkers! I'd never seen his hairy ears flap so fast. He buried his head so far into the bowl that all I could see was his tail.

"Look at that pig go!" Nana said, chomping on a plantain. "If all the food in Costa Rica tastes this good, then I'm ready to go there someday!"

"I agree with Nana," said Katie. "I can't believe that I'm saying this, but I like this stuff!"

"It's all in the spices," confessed Mom. "Mrs. Ramos even brought those over too."

How come the Ramos family had to be so nice---everyone except Marco? I just didn't understand it.

"That brings me to the big news," said Dad. "Your mom and I have decided where we're all going for summer vacation."

YES!

Katie and I held hands and crossed our fingers under the table.

"Just as long as there's a shopping mall." Katie whispered to me.

"AND a craft store with pencils!" I whispered back.

"As you know, one of the reasons I hired Dr. Ramos is so that I can take some time off and do things with the family. And this summer, we'll finally get the chance to go on a fantastic vacation!" Dad announced.

I could hardly wait. I even crossed my toes for extra luck.

"Dr. Ramos has invited us to stay at his house in Costa Rica. We'll tour the whole country!"

I'd never seen Dad so excited. That made one of us.

"Yay!!!" squealed Mom and Nana, giving each other high fives. Teeny squealed too, even though I know he didn't have a clue where Costa Rica was on a map. Come to think of it, neither did I.

I was too shocked to say anything. *What in the world was in Costa Rica?*

Why couldn't we go somewhere fun, like other normal kids? What was Dad thinking? And I SURE didn't want to stay in Marco's house!!!!

NO WAY, NO HOW, NOT IN A GAZILLION YEARS!

"What's wrong, Chan?" asked Dad. "Aren't you excited? You'll get to see lots of wild animals and butterflies. And if you're lucky, you might even see the quetzal bird!"

"The *what* bird?" I asked, grouchily.

I liked drawing birds in my sketchbook, but I'd never drawn one that I couldn't pronounce.

"The quetzal," said Nana. "I've read all about them on the internet. It's pronounced 'KET –ZAL'. They're one of the most beautiful birds in the world, but very hard to find."

That did sound sort of interesting...*sort of.* And Dad did mention wild animals and butterflies. Costa Rica might be more fun that I'd thought. Maybe I'll get a tiny bit excited.

"One more thing, Chan," Mom said. "We're also going to take Marco Ramos with us. His parents were nice enough to let him go along. Marco will show us around his home AND help us with our Spanish!"

HUH??!!

Katie let out the biggest laugh. I kicked her under the table with both feet. *What were my parents thinking?!* There was no way that I was going out of the country, out of town, or even down the street with Marco Ramos!

THIS COULD NOT BE HAPPENING!

Maybe I'll run away and join the circus. Surely someone could use an artist.

"Nana, can I spend the night with you and Teeny?" I asked nicely, hoping she'd say yes. My grandmother knew me better than anyone and she could tell I was upset with the news.

"That's a great idea, Chan. I think it's time we have some fun in the Secret Artist Hangout."

Salad Surprise

It felt good to be back at the Secret Artist Hangout. That's what Nana and I liked to call my bedroom at her house. From my snuggly stuffed animals to the yellow stars on the ceiling, it was the perfect room in every way.

I was so upset over Dad's news, that all I wanted to do was get out my sketchbook and draw. It always made me feel better. I pulled my Chocolate Brownie Brown pencil from my ponytail and drew a girl with curly hair and a pink bow.

"Mind if I come in, Chan?" asked Nana. "Would you like to talk a little? You draw, and I'll listen. How does that sound?"

Nana O'Banning always knew just what to say. I kept drawing and got out some of my other pencils.

"I don't understand why you're not tickled pink about going to Costa Rica. Your dad said we could even bring Teeny along. I'm as excited as Teeny is in a yard full of mud puddles!"

I smiled a little and kept drawing.

"I may be wrong, but it looks like you're drawing a picture of Maddy," Nana said. "How is she? I haven't seen her around lately."

I wasn't sure if I felt like talking about Maddy. I kept drawing a little longer.

"We're sort of not best friends any more. All she worries about is Marco Marco Marco. It stinks!"

Nana picked up a pencil and began drawing with me.

"Is that it? I'm sure she still wants you as her best friend, Chan. Maddy might be friends with Marco, but it's okay to be friends with lots of people."

It didn't sound okay to me. It sounded like the worst idea, ever.

"I don't know, Nana. I'll have to think about it. Maybe I should quit being mad... *maybe*."

"That's my girl. I'm sure that she's just as upset as you are, and misses you too!" Nana pointed out.

"I doubt it. Maddy's probably forgotten my name or even where I live."

"Oh fiddle faddle! The best thing to do, is talk to her about it at school," Nana said.

"And if you don't mind me saying, you need to be nice to Marco, too."

Ugh. That was pushing it.

I looked down at the letters that Nana had written at the bottom of my paper:

Channing + Maddy = Best Friends Forever.

* * *

It was finally the last week of school.

I needed every bonus point I could get in science class. I couldn't watch TV for a whole week because I'd bombed the last quiz. Dad even threatened to take my pencils away for a month.

Boring Doring put us in teams for our last project. This time he put Maddy and I together. She didn't look too happy about it, and I got a little nervous. But I kept thinking of what Nana had said at the Secret Artist Hangout.

"Class, since we're studying about plants this week, we're going to make a giant salad and study all of its parts," said our teacher. "Not only will it be a healthy snack, but you'll learn something too!"

Weird. Very weird.

"I'll give each team a vegetable that's cut into two pieces. Look at it closely and then draw its insides in your notebook."

Mr. Boring was the only one that looked excited.

"This is one strange assignment, don't you think, Maddy?" I asked, nervously.

Maddy seemed shocked that I even spoke to her. She sort of smiled back.

"Who knows, Chan. But he's coming over to our table now," she whispered. "I think we're getting the cucumber. He gave Cooper and Marco a squishy tomato. Gross!"

Did she have to bring up Marco's name again?

"Yeah, they've got a messy one. Maybe we can help them clean up after we do our drawing," I said. "Would you like me to draw a picture of the cucumber and the seeds? I don't mind."

"Sure, Chan. You're the best artist around, everyone knows that," Maddy said, smiling. "By the way, I don't have a crush on Marco anymore, but we're still friends."

"Why didn't you tell me?" I asked, shocked by the news.

"Because you never asked," said Maddy. "You only hung out with Cooper and wouldn't even talk to me."

"I thought you wanted to hang out with Marco, instead of me. Geez, Maddy, we sure got everything mixed up!" I said.

"You can say that again! Let's just forget the whole thing," said my best friend.

But I knew what I had to do next. "Since we're admitting stuff, Maddy, I got a big fat

"D" on the science quiz last week," I confessed.

"Oh, sorry Chan. But it's okay, I won't tell anyone," said Maddy. She held out her finger for a pinky promise.

Whew! What a relief. Nana was right, Maddy and I would probably be best friends forever. *Now, if I could just figure out what to do about Marco...*

ASOMBROSO! 🖉

"School's out, school's out, Teeny has a great big snout!"

Nana loved singing anytime we were about to go on vacation. And since we were traveling all the way to Costa Rica, I made sure to pack my earplugs.

After taking our seats on the plane, Nana reached into her big purse. I hoped she'd packed a bag of gummy turtles.

"Before we take off, I thought you might need a new pencil to take to Costa Rica. This one will even match your high top sneakers, Chan!"

Nana handed me a pencil with a strange name: Blue Morpho. I wasn't sure what the name meant, but I couldn't wait to use it. It matched perfectly with my blue polka dot sneakers.

"Thanks, Nana! I'll draw something cool and then mail it back to Maddy. I guess you figured out that we're best friends again. Thanks for the good advice."

I didn't tell her that Marco was still mad at me. I tried talking to him on the plane, but he just buried his head in a book. He only talked to Teeny and Katie during the whole plane ride. It was awful.

I was ready to get off the plane and go back to Greenville. Teeny didn't like being on the plane either. He kept opening and closing his mouth, so that his ears would pop. My ears hurt too and we even split a stick of gum, hoping that would help. But Teeny blew a bubble bigger than his whole head. It took forever to peel the gum out of his ears.

Once we landed in Costa Rica, Marco helped us hail a cab. At least he didn't leave me stranded at the airport.

"Taxi por favor!" yelled Marco. "Taxi por favor!"

"What's he saying?" Katie asked.

"That's Spanish for 'Taxi, please,'" I said. "Don't you know anything?"

"*Well of course* I knew that. I was just testing you!"

I knew Katie was fibbing. She'd probably been asleep during that lesson at school. I wondered if she could even count to ten.

After a short ride in the taxi, we all got into a boat and sailed up a winding river. Dad was right--this was nothing like

Greenville! I overheard Marco pronounce the name of the river for everyone. Everyone except me, that is.

"Welcome to my home. It's called *Tor-tu-ger-o* and it's named after the sea turtles. *Tortuga* is Spanish for turtle," Marco explained. "They lay eggs on the beaches at night and then hatch and go back into the ocean."

"Amazing!" Dad said.

"Asombroso!" Marco said. "That means 'amazing' in Spanish!"

As we sailed up the river, I quickly noticed something moving in the trees: MONKEYS!! They were so cute and looked just like the ones on the animal channel. They were everywhere, swinging by their tails, and making little screechy sounds.

Teeny got a little scared.

"It's okay, Teeny," said Marco, patting his head. "The spider monkeys are just curious to see us. But be careful, sometimes they like to play tricks and steal things!"

I checked to make sure that my pencil was still in my ponytail. Suddenly, I looked above my head to see a colorful bird land in the top of a tree. It looked just like the bird on a cereal box at home.

"Is that what I think it is?" asked Katie, looking through her binoculars.

"Yes, that is a toucan! We have several different species here in Costa Rica," said Marco, proudly. "And we have thousands of different plants as well. Some are even used to make medicine."

"Wow," said Katie. "I had no idea."

I had to agree with Katie. Everywhere I looked there were birds, animals, and plants—most of them I'd never seen before.

Marco had been right all along.

I couldn't wait to unpack my suitcase and get out my sketchbook. Luckily, Mom brought along a camera. The birds wouldn't sit still long enough for me to draw them.

Marco introduced us to his aunt and uncle, and his cousin, Tica. She looked about the same age as Marco and I.

"Welcome to Costa Rica," said Tica's mom. "We're glad to have you visit our beautiful country. We've heard lots about you."

"Are you really an artist?" asked Tica. "I like art stuff too."

"Awesome!" I said, wondering what else Marco had told her. "I like to draw with colored pencils."

"I paint with watercolors," said Tica. "Maybe I'll show you some of my paintings later."

At least I could get along with someone in Marco's family.

"Tomorrow we'll hike into the cloud forest and try to find the famous quetzal," said

Marco's uncle. "Who knows, we may get lucky!"

"Yippee!!" said Nana. "I've been wanting to see that bird for years!"

"Then we'll have to look extra hard. Get some rest everyone! Cloud forest, here we come!"

I was too excited to sleep and could hear the animals howling in the jungle. But there was one thing that kept bugging me: *What on earth was a cloud forest??*

Weird. Very weird.

Oh Why Did
I Do That?!

"Oh Channn.......Katieeee......up and at it you two...time to get up! The birds are waiting!" Nana said.

I rolled over and looked at the clock: *6:00 AM?!*

Great gorillas! Why did we have to get up so early?

Katie's snoring had been loud enough to wake up every monkey in the jungle. I hadn't slept a wink.

"Nana, do you know what time it is?" I asked. "I thought we were on vacation? Katie's snoring sounded like your car--- *after* the muffler fell off!"

I buried my head under my pillow, but Nana ignored my whining. She even sent Teeny in after us. He pranced in, grabbed my blanket, and pulled it off the bed with one jerk. I guess he was ready to go too.

"Okay, okay, you hyper pig! I'm up, I'm up!"

Katie still hadn't moved a muscle and Teeny knew it. He quietly walked over and licked her across the mouth.

"EWWW! GROSS, TEENY! I probably need a tetanus shot now! The last thing I need around here is pig slobber! Thanks for waking me up in the yuckiest way ever!"

After throwing on some clothes, I quickly stuck my Blue Morpho pencil into my pony-tail and laced up my zebra striped sneakers.

I grabbed my sketchbook, put the binoculars around my neck, and headed towards the jeep. I felt like a real jungle explorer.

Katie, on the other hand, was more interested in covering every inch of her body with bug spray.

"Have you seen the SIZE of the mosquitos around here?" she asked. "They're big enough to carry Teeny away! Everyone better use this stuff!"

Marco and his uncle were already awake too. Tica was helping them put stuff into the jeep.

"Hey Marco," I said, trying to be nice, "does your family get up early like this all the time?"

I could tell that he was still mad at me.

"It's best to go bird watching early, since they're more active then. But I forgot, Channing O'Banning, you don't believe anything that I say!"

Marco stomped off to the jeep. I guess I deserved it since I laughed at his story about the blue jean frog. I shouldn't have made fun of him at school, even though I knew he'd made up the whole silly thing. Maybe he was just trying to fit in or something.

"Okay gang, we're off to the cloud forest!" yelled Dad.

"Here's a photo of a quetzal, or ket-zal," said Tica. "Their tail looks like a long green fern. It helps them hide in the jungle."

I looked closer at the photo. "Wow, it looks like their feathers have been painted with a paint brush!"

If only I could be the first person to spot one in the cloud forest. I made sure that my pencils were sharpened in my backpack, just in case I got lucky.

"Why is the place we're going to called the cloud forest?" I asked.

"That's a very good question, Channing O'Banning," said Marco's uncle. "It's very misty and really damp up there---sort of like being in the clouds. The quetzal bird likes to live in that environment. So do tons of other animals.

"What *kind* of other animals?" asked Katie, turning pale as a ghost. "Anything d-d-d-dangerous?"

"There are all kinds of bats, sloths, and howler monkeys. And if we're lucky, we might even see a jaguar!" Marco said.

"Uh...I...I think I'll just stay in the jeep!" said Katie.

My sister didn't look so good. Her face was kind of green.

"There's even an animal called a peccary," said Marco. "It looks like a strange pig."

"Fantastico!" giggled Nana. "Teeny, you may find your long lost cousin!"

After riding in the jeep for a while, we hiked up a large mountain. My legs felt like limp noodles. Everything became so damp that my shirt stuck to my skin. My hair felt glued to my head. This had to be the cloud forest!

I remembered Boring Doring telling us that the top of the jungle was called the canopy. We looked everywhere for the quetzal. Each time that Mom thought she'd spotted one in the canopy, it was a green fern instead.

"Psst...Channing, come quick," whispered Nana, up ahead of me. "But be very very quiet..."

Maybe it was a quetzal or some other strange bird! I double-checked my ponytail to make sure that I had my pencil. When I got closer, I saw a huge butterfly that was bright yellow. Greenville had butterflies, but nothing like this.

"It's called a Yellow Swallowtail, Chan. Isn't it stunning?" said Nana.

She tiptoed over quickly and took a photo. But I was determined to draw the butterfly while it sat on a flower. Just when I was about to get closer, it flew to another flower... and then another....and then another. If I could just keep up with it for a few more seconds, I'd have a great drawing for Maddy.

But then something horrible happened.

I followed the swallowtail so far into the jungle that I got away from the others. All of the paths and tree branches started to look alike.

I was lost in the cloud forest!

And to make things worse, the only person who knew *anything* about the jungle, wouldn't even speak to me. Marco probably hoped I'd stay lost forever. I yelled for Nana...for Dad...even for Marco.

No one answered.

Is That What I Think It Is?

Every tree looked the same. What if I was walking in circles? What if I never got out of the cloud forest? What if a spider monkey stole all of my colored pencils?

I didn't know where to turn and decided to sit down on a rock and think. Mom always told me that if I ever had a tough choice to make, to stop and really think about it *slowly*. I doubt if she was talking about getting lost in the rainforest of Costa Rica, but what choice did I have?

Suddenly I heard something: "chirrrrp... chirpppp..."

It sounded like a cricket or a frog. Maybe it was a MONSTER frog that would eat me--- just like the one in my nightmare!!! My knees began knocking as I saw something jump high out of a plant. At least it looked tiny.

I tiptoed over to get a closer look.

I blinked my eyes to make sure that I wasn't seeing things. It was a...a...BLUE... JEAN...FROG! Its body was the brightest red I'd ever seen and it's legs were the color of blue jeans! Great gorillas! Marco was telling the truth!

Ugh, did I feel dumb! Now I *really* had to tell Marco I was sorry. I couldn't believe that I was staring at a blue jean frog. I quickly got out my sketchbook and drew it before it jumped away.

"Oh Channnnn...Channing O'Banning... Can you hear me...Channnnn?"

I knew that voice!

"Dad! Dad! I'm over here! Over here!" I yelled, so excited to hear him.

Soon I saw Mom, Dad and Katie running towards me. Whew! I thought I'd never see them again!

Nana, Teeny, and Marco weren't far behind.

"Thank goodness we found you!" Mom cried. "Don't you ever scare us like that again! I thought I'd lost my little artist."

"Yeah, you goofy kid," said Katie. "next time, take a compass."

As we made our way back to the jeep, I stayed close to Mom and walked beside Marco.

"Uh, Marco...I think I owe you an apology," I said. "I really goofed up."

Marco was speechless. I think he was in shock.

"I should have believed you at school," I admitted. "While I was lost in the jungle, I actually saw a blue jean frog. I almost didn't believe it, but I saw it with my very own eyes."

"See, I told you, Chan! Aren't they cool looking?" asked Marco, smiling from ear to ear.

"Totally cool looking!" I agreed. "And, Marco, you know LOTS more about plants and animals than I ever will. Maybe next year you can help me in science class. It's not one of my best subjects."

"Sure, Chan, no problem," Marco said, and then gave me a fist bump. "We've got one more thing to do before we leave the cloud forest----ZIP LINE!!!!"

Marco ran on ahead. I had no clue what "zip line" meant, but I knew now to trust my friend. Everyone was given a helmet to wear and a harness to strap around their waist. Even Nana and Teeny wore one.

This could be tricky.

Marco went first and hooked his harness to a long rope that went from one tree all the way over to another. It was far, far away.

In one jump and loud scream, Marco zoomed across the top of the jungle, stopping way over on the other side. It looked just like he was flying through the trees! Tica went next, and she flew faster than Marco.

"Yippee!! Teeny and I want to go next!" I yelled, getting in line. "Hold on tight, you wild and crazy pig!"

With one big push, Teeny and I flew across the zip line and squealed at the top of our lungs. It was AWESOME! Zip lining was the most fun I'd ever had on any summer vacation! Katie was the last one to come across and closed her eyes the entire way.

Just as we were taking off our helmets, Marco froze in his tracks. *What was wrong with him? Was he sick?*

"Sshhhh. Sshhhhh. Quiet everyone," he whispered.

Marco grabbed his binoculars and looked up into the canopy. I quickly did as Marco and looked up into the trees.

"What is it Marco...is it...a *quetzal*?" I whispered, trying not to scream.

"Hold on...I think...I think...IT IS! You're right Channing!" said Marco. Everyone hurried to look through their binoculars.

"It's more beautiful than I ever imagined. Look at the shades of green....and red...and yellow!" said Nana. "What an amazing creature!"

"Asombroso!" Marco and I said at the same time. We couldn't help but giggle at having the very same thought. It shouldn't have been *that* surprising--good friends think alike lots of times!

Stinkville

The more I talked with Marco, the more I could see why he and Maddy were friends. He was really nice—*even if he was a boy.*

After making our way out of the cloud forest, we hopped back into the jeep and headed to a new place. Marco and I sat in the back-seat and looked at a book called *Wild Plants of the Tropical Rainforest.*

"How come your country has such strange names for everything?" I asked. "I can't even pronounce the name of the place we're going to next."

"They're not strange to me," Marco said. "They're Spanish words that we're used to saying. If you ask me, I think Greenville sounds strange, especially the name of that street you live on. What's it called again?"

"Darcy Street," I reminded him. "What's strange about that? I guess it all depends on where you grow up, huh? What's the name of the place we're going to now?"

"It's called *AR-E-NAL* and it's awesome. There's a huge lake--- and a volcano!"

That's when Katie freaked out again.

"A VOLCANO?" she asked. "Excuse me, but WHY are we going there? I'd like to live to graduate from high school---not drown in a molten pool of lava!"

"It's okay, Katie," said Tica. "We'll be far away. But it does have orange lava that flows out of it lots of times. It looks cool at night--like the mountain is glowing."

"I can't wait to see it!" I chimed in. "Instead of studying about a volcano in Mr. Boring's class, we can see the real thing!"

"Sí, sí, Channing!" said Marco, "I told you that Costa Rica is a pretty awesome place."

"Sí, sí, Marco!" I said.

Katie was right, even though I hated to admit it: It was much easier getting along with Marco than being mad at him.

After driving up and over several mountains, Marco's uncle finally stopped the jeep. I didn't see a volcano or a lake anywhere.

Weird. Very weird.

"Okay, time for everyone to get out again," said Dad. "Grab your binoculars and your plant book. Let's go into the jungle and explore a little!"

I wanted to see the volcano----not more plants in the jungle. I already got lost once and wasn't ready for a repeat.

Katie began spraying herself from head to toe again with her gross-smelling bug spray. Why was she acting so bonkers over a few little bugs? The huge cloud of spray caused me to choke. Even Teeny was gasping for air.

"Katie! Enough of the spray, already!" I yelled. "No bug is going to come CLOSE to you! But that fog of stink might kill the rest of us!"

Katie totally ignored me and followed behind Nana into the rainforest. There was something different about the ferns, plants, and trees around here. They smelled so good and looked nothing like the ones in Greenville. As I followed behind Mom and Dad, they quickly came to a stop beside a large tree with tiny flowers at the bottom.

"Katie... Nana...the rest of you come and see this too," said Dad.

We all gathered near the tree and looked at the leaves and bark.

"This is the Cin-chona tree," said Marco's uncle. "Its bark is used for medicine to treat malaria."

"What's malaria?" I asked. I didn't remember Dad ever mentioning it at home.

"It's a disease that's spread in very warm climates. It's actually spread by mosquitos and can cause people to get really sick. But thanks to the rainforest, we have medicine that helps!"

"SEE, I told you!" squealed Katie, "I KNEW I'd need more bug spray around here!"

Here comes stinkville.

I tried breathing through my mouth so I wouldn't inhale Katie's fumes.

It was strange that something like tree bark could be used in medicine. Marco had told us that living in Costa Rica was like having a pharmacy in the backyard. Now I knew what he meant.

Marco walked past me and over to a bunch of pink flowers. Was he going to pick flowers for me? I hope he didn't think I wanted to be his girlfriend!

"Hey, Chan, over here. I want to show you something," he said. "These are Madagascar Rosy Periwinkles. This plant helps fight cancer. Pretty cool, huh?"

"I'll say! Does everything in the rainforest do something amazing?"

"It sure seems that way," he said. "Like my Dad always says, everything has a purpose, even plants. It's too bad that they're disappearing."

"What? *Disappearing?*" I asked, confused.

"Yeah. Every year, thousands of acres of the rainforest are cut down. Some people want the land for farming or to have land for cattle. They call it deforestation."

"That's crazy, Marco! Don't they know how important these plants are?" I asked, shocked.

"I wish that were true. But it's hard to convince everyone."

"Hey kids, check out this view!" yelled Nana. She'd gone up ahead and had hiked a little higher.

Then we saw it: Arenal Volcano. Although it was far away, it still looked huge and was oozing with lava. I couldn't imagine how hot it was up there. It could probably cook an egg in two seconds!

"Isn't that one of the most beautiful things you've ever seen?" sighed Nana.

Marco and Tica were right. It looked like the mountain was glowing.

Even Katie was speechless.

Birds of a Feather ......

Grrr.....gloop....grrp.

My stomach was going crazy. Even though we saw lots of cool stuff in the rainforest, I didn't see anything that looked tasty.

"Isn't it time for lunch? I'm starving!" I said.

"I second that," said Katie. "I'm so hungry that I could even eat one of those goofy gummy turtles."

After driving a little further, Marco's uncle finally stopped at a small restaurant.

"I hope the O'Banning girls like burritos," he said. "This place has the best around!"

I LOVED burritos and so did Katie. Maybe she'd get extra flaming hot sauce on hers by mistake. Now *that* would be funny.

When we sat down at the table, I noticed something really odd. The restaurant owner had oranges and grapefruits cut in half and hanging by strings outside.

"What's with the oranges on a string?" I asked Marco. "That's the strangest thing ever."

"YOU'RE the strangest thing, ever!" Katie said.

She was back to her old self again. If only a mosquito could have bitten her on the lip.

"These oranges are feeders," Marco said. "Cooh, huh?"

"Feeders? What kind of animals eat oranges and grapefruits hanging on a string?" asked Katie. "Is it a TIGER? If it is, then I'm outta here! Bring my burrito to the jeep!"

Katie was clueless, but so was I.

Suddenly, a green and purple hummingbird zoomed right above my head. It went straight to an orange and then on to the grapefruit. Its wings fluttered so fast that I could barely see them move. Then another hummingbird came...and three more after that. They sounded like a swarm of bumblebees.

"Oh my!" said Mom. "They're everywhere! Quick, someone, take a photo of these!"

Dad snapped his camera, and I grabbed my sketchbook. It was a good thing that my Pookie Purple was in my ponytail! I drew a tiny green hummingbird with a purple spot under its chin.

"That's a really good drawing," said Marco. "After we finish eating, I have another surprise for you."

What could Marco be up to this time? I'd already seen plants, frogs, and tons of birds. What else could there be in Costa Rica?

"The owner of the restaurant is a friend of ours," said Marco. "He has a very interesting garden out back."

What was so special about a garden? We had those at Greenville. I even helped Nana with hers sometimes.

Just when I was ready to ask Marco about it, my crazy sister squealed and began packing her mouth with ice. She looked like a gerbil.

"YEOWWWW!! My mouth is on FIRE!!! What on earth is in that burrito, Marco?!" asked Katie, fanning her mouth with a napkin. "I feel like I just ate the sun!"

Even Marco couldn't help but giggle. "A glass of milk always cools down spicy food. Would you like me to get you some, Katie?"

"Forget the glass!" she mumbled. "I'll take the whole cow!"

* * *

I couldn't wait to see what was so different about a garden in Costa Rica. Marco pointed to a small table with tiny glass bottles sitting on top. This garden was already a weird one.

"Hola. Hello!" said a man filling up the bottles with red water, "Have you come to feed my birds for me?"

"We have," said Marco. "This is Mr. Hernandez, everyone."

"And these are our friends, the O'Bannings," said Tica.

"Buenos dias," I said.

"Good day to you too!" said Mr. Hernandez. "Watch what happens if you sit here and hold the bottle like this."

All of the sudden, a hummingbird zoomed in and sat right on my finger! It stuck its long beak into the bottle and drank the red water inside. I looked over at Nana, and one was eating out of her bottle too.

"Wow! Whatever this stuff is, it must be good."

"It's a type of sugar water," said Mr. Hernandez. "And the red color reminds them of flowers in the jungle."

"They must have a sweet tooth!" said Katie. "It does look kind of tasty."

"Don't get any ideas," I giggled. "You need to stick with flaming burritos!"

Time to Fly ✏

It was our last day in Costa Rica, and I
didn't want to go home. Even Katie wanted
to stay longer. I had no idea that Costa Rica
would be such a fun place to visit.

"We have one more surprise before head-
ing to the airport!" said Marco.

"Come on, give us a hint," I said.

"Yeah, Marco, just a tiny one," said Katie.

"Okay, okay. Our last stop is a farm and
that's all I'm going to say."

A farm? That's our last stop in Costa Rica?

"What do they grow there? I hope they grow mangos like we ate yesterday. Those things were DE-LISH!" said Katie.

"Sorry," said Marco, "I don't think so. You'll just have to wait and see."

"Are we going to a coffee plantation, Marco?" I asked. "I read that Costa Rica grows lots of coffee. I think coffee tastes like liquid dirt, but Mom lives on the stuff."

"Wrong again. Sorry, Chan. But we're almost there so you won't have to keep guessing!"

As we pulled into the driveway of the farm, I noticed there wasn't a barn, or animals, or anything. The only thing that I saw was a large greenhouse.

"Are we at a flower farm, Marco? Is that it?"

"You're getting closer," he hinted. "Something like that."

"Well let's quit playing guessing games, you silly kids!" said Nana. "Come on, Teeny, let's find out what this last stop is all about! We'll beat them to it."

Nana had only been inside a few minutes when she came running out to find me. Teeny ran back to the jeep faster than a cheetah. He began poking me with his snout like it was some kind of emergency.

"Calm down, you silly pig!" I laughed and said. "What is wrong with you? Have you been drinking Mom's coffee?"

"Channing O'Banning! You'll never guess what's inside that greenhouse!" Nana said, jumping up and down. "You'll want to get that pencil I bought you for the trip! Hurry now, stick it in your ponytail!"

Nana wasn't making any sense, but I did as she asked. I stuck my blue pencil into my ponytail and made sure that my sketchbook was in my backpack. The front door read "Blue Morpho Farm."

I still didn't understand. *Blue Morpho?* I looked in my plant book but didn't see it anywhere. That was also the name of the pencil that Nana had given me.

"You're wasting your time looking in that book," said Marco. "Why don't you open the door and go inside?"

Teeny pushed me forward with his snout and I looked up at the ceiling. I could hardly believe my eyes: BUTTERFLIES!!

It was a butterfly farm!!

"Wow!" said Katie. "This is incredible! I've never seen so many butterflies in my entire life! They're everywhere!"

Katie was right. It was a sea of blue fluttering wings.

"I told you it was a farm! Just different," said Marco. "Costa Rica has over three thousand species of butterflies."

"Hi everyone, my name is Mr. Albarez. Welcome to the Blue Morpho Butterfly Farm!

Can you see why it's called the most beautiful butterfly on earth? We have them in all stages to help you understand their development."

I quickly grabbed my Blue Morpho pencil from my ponytail and drew what was in front of me.

Teeny went crazy trying to chase them. One butterfly even landed on his tail!

"Here is the butterfly in the caterpillar stage. We try to protect them so they aren't eaten by birds."

Mr. Albarez pointed to several plump little worms hanging onto plant leaves. They didn't look anything like butterflies.

"These caterpillars will eat, turn white, and go through a molting stage," he said. "Then, at eleven weeks, each one hangs upside down and turns into a *chrysalis*."

I had no idea that becoming a butterfly was so much work!

"And in just two weeks, the blue morpho appears like magic," said Marco. "Isn't it strange how they go through all of those stages?"

Their wings were the prettiest blue I'd ever seen. They almost glowed.

"I guess we all change in our own way," said Nana. "I've always heard that if a butterfly lands on you, it means that you're beautiful! I sure hope one lands on me!"

Within minutes, the butterflies had landed on all of us. Teeny was covered in butterflies from snout to tail! He smiled from ear to ear when Nana took his picture. I couldn't wait to go to the gift shop.

Dad bought me a cool T-shirt with a blue morpho on the back. When I tried it on, it looked just like I had wings. I even bought one for Maddy. She liked butterflies as much as I did.

Going Green??

We finally made it to the airport and I felt sort of sad. Still, I could hardly wait to tell Maddy and Cooper about everything---especially the blue jean frog. It was a good thing that I drew it in my sketchbook.

I could tell it that it was tough for Marco to say goodbye, too. Greenville was far away, and I'm sure he wondered when he'd be back to see his family.

"It's okay, Marco," I said, trying to make him feel better. "I'm sure you'll come back again. Maybe they can fly to Greenville one of these days."

Tica overheard us talking and couldn't help but join in.

"Sí, sí, Channing O'Banning! I would LOVE to visit America! Maybe my father will let me come and stay with Marco during vacation!"

Tica handed me a small present wrapped in a banana leaf and tied with a ribbon.

"It's a small gift to say thank you for visiting my country."

I untied the ribbon to find two new colored pencils! One was called Rainforest Green and the other was Periwinkle Pink. I stuck both of them into my ponytail.

"Now you can draw the rainforest anytime you'd like!" said Tica. "And tell your friends to help preserve the jungle! Our plants and animals can use all the help they can get!"

"Sí, sí !" I yelled back. "I'll tell them, Tica. Gracias!"

After taking our seats on the plane, I got out my sketchbook and tried out my new pencils. I drew a picture of Tica and Marco zip lining through the rainforest. I was going to make double sure that my friends in Greenville knew why the rainforest was so important. Marco even said he'd help me.

Teeny cuddled under a blanket, and snored louder than Katie. Nana had her head buried in a book called *Going Green Made Easy*.

"That's sure a weird title," I said. "What's it about?"

"It's all about how to go green. Visiting Costa Rica made me realize how important it really is."

Going green? What did that mean?

I wasn't sure what Nana was talking about.

Weird. Very weird.

"Sorry Nana, but I don't understand," I admitted. "When I didn't put on enough sunscreen at the beach, I turned really pink. But I've never heard of anyone turning green."

Nana smiled and turned to one of the pages in her book.

"Going green means doing any little thing you can to help protect the environment. Don't you think it's important to keep our earth as healthy as possible?"

"Sure Nana," I admitted. "But I wouldn't even know where to start."

"Well this book says that every little thing counts. Recycling is an easy way to start. We can recycle plastic, paper, even glass." Nana continued.

"Makes sense to me!" I said. "Marco mentioned that people are cutting down trees in the rainforest, in order to have more land. Don't they realize that they're destroying animals' homes--AND destroying medicine that we need?!"

"I wish that they did," said Nana. "We need to protect our animals *and* our rainforests."

Nana was right. Maybe I'd go green too.

"What else can we do at home, besides recycling?" I asked, looking into her book.

"All sorts of things! We can try to save water at home. Do you keep the water running when you're brushing your teeth?"

"I keep it running," I said, feeling bad. "That's wasting water, huh?"

"I'm afraid so. And do you turn off the lights upstairs, when you leave the Secret Artist Hangout?"

"No, sorry, Nana," I admitted. "I guess I'm not very green, huh?"

"Not very green YET," she said. "But we can change that when we get back home. Sound good?"

"Sounds ASOMBROSO! That's *amazing* in Spanish, remember?"

"What's amazing is that Marco helped rescue you in the rainforest, and now you can help rescue the rainforest with Marco," said Nana. "Like you always say, Channing O'Banning, that's weird. Very weird!"

Green in Greenville

It felt good to be back at my house on Darcy Street. Katie was glad too, since she didn't have to coat herself in bug spray anymore. As soon as we carried everything inside, I called Maddy and Cooper to come over.

"Finally, you're back home!" said Maddy, running up the stairs.

"Yeah, Greenville was totally boring without you here, Channing O'Banning!" Cooper said. "I got so bored that I even read about the rainforest on the computer. From what I read on those websites, you're lucky you made it back in one piece!"

"Sure I'm fine, silly. Costa Rica is the coolest place EVER. There were all sorts of beautiful frogs, birds, and insects," I said. "Oh, and Marco wasn't too bad, either."

Maddy looked at me like I was an alien.

"YOU got along with MARCO? And now you think that a frog is BEAUTIFUL? Did you leave your brain in the jungle?" Maddy asked.

I got out my sketchbook and showed them some of my drawings. Then we got on the computer and looked at Dad's photos.

"Wow, these are awesome, Chan!" said Maddy. "You need to bring these to class when school starts back. Boring Doring might even put them on the bulletin board."

Did Maddy have to remind me? I'd tried blocking Boring Doring out of my head for the summer. But after visiting Costa Rica, I could see why he went cuckoo over plants.

"That's a cool t-shirt you're wearing," said Cooper, "but that is one WEIRD looking butterfly on the back."

"I think it's beautiful," said Maddy. "Are they really that blue?"

"No," I smiled, "they're even bluer! They're called Blue Morpho butterflies and I brought you both back a souvenir."

I handed Maddy a t-shirt, just like mine. Now we looked like twins.

"This is my new favorite shirt, Channing O'Banning! Let's wear them on the first day of school!"

I handed Cooper a small can with a lid on top. Inside was a plant with a fat green caterpillar. Cooper looked confused.

"Uh, thanks Chan...*I guess,*" Coop looked down into the can and crinkled his nose. "But what am I supposed to do with a...a... *worm?*"

Cooper didn't understand...YET!

"This is only the first stage, but in a few weeks it will turn into a beautiful blue morpho butterfly!

"No way!" said Cooper.

"You mean a real, live butterfly will be in there?" asked Maddy, looking into the can.

"Just make sure it has food. It should change in a few weeks!"

I told them about the butterfly farm and zip lining through the jungle. Cooper really liked hearing about the plants that treat diseases.

"The only thing we have in our backyard are weeds," said Cooper. "I doubt if they do anything, except make me sneeze."

"The only plant that I know about is POISON IVY," Maddy said. "But maybe there's a plant in the rainforest that makes it quit itching like crazy!"

"Probably so," I said, "but the rainforest is disappearing and that's a BIG problem! My Nana says that we need to go green."

"Huh?" asked Cooper. "You're back to acting all goofy again, Channing."

"TA DA!!!!" I said, flipping open my sketchbook. "May I present the amazing list of How To Go Green!"

Maddy and Coop were clueless but that was about to change.

Paper or Plastic?

"Okay, let's hear it," sighed Cooper, "but sometimes, Channing O'Banning, your plans are a little... well...*out there.*"

"Yeah, and sometimes they end up being a major disaster!" Maddy said. "Remember the Greenville Pet Show? We had animals running all over the school! I even got FLEAS!"

"Shhh! Don't even mention that," said Cooper. "You'll make me feel creepy crawly all over again! I still have nightmares about that kid in second grade with the pet rat. Why would anyone want such a thing?"

"Going green means doing stuff every day to save water or electricity. It keeps our earth clean."

"Oh, so that's it!" said Cooper, "I think my dad is going green at home. He has our trash divided up in the kitchen. He has one bag for paper and one for plastic. At first, I thought he was practicing to be a garbage man."

"He's being smart and recycling," I said. "If he takes the stuff to a recycling center, it can be made into something else. Otherwise it ends up in a big trash landfill."

"Land filled with TRASH?? Now *that* would be totally gross!" said Maddy. "What can I do to be green?"

"You can turn off the lights when you're not using them," I said. "And you could walk to school or ride with us, instead of having your mom drive her car."

"That sounds simple enough." said Maddy.

"Hey, dad said something like that too. If we reduce the number of cars, then that's less carbon and smelly junk in the air." Cooper added.

Maddy was in deep thought about what I'd just said.

"Are you sure you didn't hit your head on one of those banana trees? You're not the same, Channing O'Banning."

"Sure I am, Maddy," I said. "I'm just a little smarter, thanks to Marco and Costa Rica. We need to talk about my plan to save the rainforest, too. I've got lots of cool ideas on how to stop deforestation. Did you know that Marco is a genius when it comes to plants?"

Maddy and Cooper looked at each other and rolled their eyes.

"It's just too weird. When you left for vacation, you couldn't stand Marco!" Cooper said. "If only that crazy pig of your Nana's could talk. Maybe he could explain what's happened to you."

"Let's just say I was a little lost," I admitted. "Marco's pretty cool when you get to know him. He's even going to help us with a "Go Green in Greenville" plan when school starts back. Will you help us?"

"We're best friends aren't we?" asked Maddy. "But please, no fleas this time!"

"Count me in too," said Cooper, smiling. "Because I have a feeling you'll make me help anyway."

Coop was right. Maybe he'd even blab and tell the whole school about it!

This time, I didn't mind at all.

THE END

Want to learn more about Channing
O'Banning?
Find out where the famous fourth grade
artist is going next!
Check out www.channingobanning.com